CW00404369

T.M. Cooks is the pen name of the following collaborative writing team. The contributors are:

- Liam Vincent

- Fraya Parks

- John Frazer

- Amelia Bettridge

- Harley Duke

- Niamh Talbott

- Charlotte King

- Lewis Ball

- Jackson Bannister

The project was overseen by Joe Reddington, Dr Yvonne Skipper and Richard Seymour.

The group cheerfully acknowledges the wonderful help given by:

- Emma Berry-Dinnage

- Lucy Dukes

And a big thank you goes to Higher Horizons who funded this wonderful project. Its been a wonderful opportunity, and everyone involved has been filled with incredible knowledge and enthusiasm. Finally, we would like to thank all staff at Tamworth Enterprise College for their support in releasing our novelists from lessons for a full week.

The group started to plan out their novel at 9.15 on Monday 11 December 2023 and completed their last proofreading at 14.00 on Friday 15 December 2023.

We are incredibly proud to state that every word of the story, every idea, every chapter and yes, every mistake, is entirely their own work. No teachers, parents or other students touched a single key during this process, and we would ask readers to keep this in mind. We are sure you will agree that this is an incredible achievement. It has been a true delight and privilege to see this group of young people turn into professional novelists in front of our very eyes.

Reign of Chaos: The Second Fall

T. M. Cooks

Contents

Chapter 1

Prologue

All was void. There was no concept

of time, space, colour. For years, decades even, there was no sound; no white noise of birds chirping, no smell, no anything. There was nothing at all inside of this void except a dot. One small dot.

This small dot exploded into massive spheres as hot as magma, but as light as a cloud. All over this void, some of these spheres collapsed into massive oceans of light and these oceans of light produced small balls of bright colours of all different shapes and sizes. One of these balls was called Earth and was coloured blue and green, with vast oceans, varied life, tall mountains and most importantly, magic. Yes, it's true. This blue and green ball of life had the power of magic in it's dirt. That was until the Great War between Heaven and Hell. God and Satan had made an agreement for magic to be banished from Earth and into space. That was until . . . Archangel Gabriel.

-

Chapter 2

The Suitcase

Sarah was in her Mom's car on the way

to a new beginning. She was so excited, but at the same time really nervous and couldn't stop thinking about university and missing her sister, Una. Anxiously, she tapped the plastic casing of her suitcase with her hand.

Reassuringly, her mother said, "Don't worry, it's fine to be nervous on your first day at university. When I was your age, I was so nervous that my dad had to pull me out of the car door just to get me out of the car. Oh, those were the good days."

"OK, Mom", Sarah replied, rolling her eyes ever so slightly at her mother's words, even though she was still incredibly nervous. "Did you miss your siblings when you went to university?"

"Oh, yes I did. I missed them so much that I would have just put them in my suit-

case and brought them with me if I could,
" Sarah's Mom chuckled.

Sarah chuckled, then sighed as the car
stopped. She got out of the car and hauled
the huge, heavy suitcase out of the boot.
It felt like it was full of bricks it was so
heavy, and Sarah could have sworn it was
not that heavy when they had left.

I must have packed more than I thought.

Saying goodbye to her Mom, she pulled
the heavy suitcase inside of the university, having to take deep breaths and short
breaks along the way. When she finally
found her room, she placed her suitcase
onto her bed and unzipped it, only to find
her sister, Una, curled up in a ball inside
of the suitcase!

"Una!?" she said with confusion and
surprise dwelling in her voice. "What are

you doing in my suitcase?" She sounded angry, her concern getting the better of her.

"I just wanted to surprise you, did you like the surprise?" Una replied with a big grin over her face.

"Yes, it is a very nice surprise, but how did you get in there? And since you are here can you please help me unpack?"

When they finished talking, Una helped Sarah unpack and decorate her room and calmed Sarah down.

"Thank you, Una, for helping me unpack." Sarah gave her sister a warm smile, "But now i need to go and sign in to my university account and go to the lecture in the main hall for the new students such as myself. So you stay here. Ok?"

"Ok! Good luck!", Replied Una with a

cute smile.

Chapter 3

Taken

Una looked around her sister's brand

15

new university room. It was small, but bright and there were lots of shelves where she imagined Sarah would put all of her dance trophies. Sarah was amazing at dance. She was amazing at most things she tried and Una looked up to her because of this. She was the best big sister, and the thought of her leaving had been too devastating. All Una had wanted to do was follow Sarah, and so she had.

Alone in the room, Una decided that she would search through Sarah's stuff just to make sure she packed everything she needed. As she was sorting through a heap of boring old clothes, she thought she had heard a rustle in the corner of the room, but thought nothing of it. It was probably just someone in the corridor.

She felt like she had won the lottery after she found Sarah's Nintendo. She began to play on it, but was quickly stopped by a student ambassador standing in the corner of the room.

"Hello there!" The student ambassador said with a cheerful smile. "Would you like to come with me, so I can interest you with some clubs that I can guarantee you will enjoy?"

Una nodded and placed the Nintendo down. She walked over to the student ambassador and asked, "Are there any art clubs?" Una started putting her sisters shoes on (although they were way too big for her).

"I should hope so!" The student ambassador said with a smirk that told nothing but lies.

"Just before we go can we wait for my

17

sister? I need her approval."

"NO I NEED YOU NOW!"

The student ambassador pulled out a knife and held it to Una's neck. Una's eyes widened.

"What's your name little child?" She said, looking like a psychopath.

"M-My n-name i-is Una..." Una's eyes started tearing up as she wished for her sister to come back.

"How old are you?" The student ambassador asked and noticed Una's eyes tearing up.

"I-I'm Th-thirteen and a half..." She said as she looked at the knife and back at the student ambassador's face.

"My name is Amaris and I'll be your kidnapper for the week, " Amaris said whilst moving the knife to Una's back. "Do you love your sister, Una?"

Amaris tightened her grip around Una with great strength. Una dodged knocking clothes around the room, but Amaris grabbed her arm.

"H-how do you know about my sister?" Una said with a single tear rolling down her face.

"Asrani... My 'friend', " Amaris said with a grimace while she led Una out of the building. The knife poked Una in the back "Answer my question!"

"I love my sister with all my heart..." Una said, smiling at the thought.

"Perfect, " Amaris muttered under her breath. Amaris then put a gag inside Una's mouth to keep her quiet.

They disappeared out of the school's campus and down to a cave with stairs.

19

Amaris went to push Una down the stairs, but thought otherwise she would probably do something better.

Amaris trudged down flights of stairs with Una still in front of her. Holding the knife to her spine, she kicked Una attempting to make her tumble down the stairs but it didn't work and she just tripped. Amaris curses under her breath and takes a deep breath.

"HURRY UP!" Amaris shouts at Una. Una jumps and rushes down the five flights of stairs breathing rapidly.

"Why are you doing this to me!?" Una blurts out,

"I'm sick of seeing happy relationships! I want my own for once!", "And I will get it when the ritual is complete!" she smirks smugly. Una started to cry, she sniffled

20

and wiped her eyes with her arm making her tears drip down her skin." Where are you taking me, you imbecile?!" Una had spat out the gag, so Amaris had to cover her mouth. Una squirmed to escape but failed.

"Stop moving, you little brat!" Amaris poked her in the back with the knife again. "Keep squirming and I'll throw you down these stairs like you're a ragdoll!"

"O-Okay I'll stop, " Una said whilst trying to kick Amaris.

"DO YOU WANT ME TO THROW YOU DOWN THE STAIRS?!" she asked loudly as she grabbed Una's head and placed it forcefully on the railings.

"Please don't..." Una said, suddenly very scared at the display of anger. Amaris lifted Una's head off the railings and started walking down the staircase. She cursed under her breath and continued walking down the staircase.

They reached the bottom of the stairs and Amaris was practically dragging Una behind her.

"It's not sleepy time just yet, Una, " Amaris sing-songed as she tugged at Una's hair and decided to drag Una by the hair to her designated area. She slapped Una awake.

"Put this on and make it quick!" Amaris threw some grey and white striped clothing to Una.

"Do you have it in purple?" She asked. Amaris shook her head in a disapproving way.

"What about in pink?" Una asked, looking hopeful. Amaris looked like she was about to strangle Una with the clothes she was refusing to wear.

"No, we don't have it in pink." Amaris said while fighting the urge to shout at her. "Will you just put the damn clothes on and then we can get this over and done with!" Amaris yelled walking out of the room leaving Una to change.

After Una had changed, Amaris rolled her eyes.

"Took you long enough, " Amaris said with annoyance as she dragged Una by the arm into the bright lights of the laboratory. Instead of stopping there, she went through some double doors and down some more stairs until they reached a giant pentagram. "This is where you will be staying!" Amaris told Una.

"Ew... do you have any more rooms

available?" Una asked, as she was looking around the room with a dissatisfied look on her face. Amaris shook her head and tied Una up ready for what was about to happen.

Chapter 4

Death Is Near

Sarah walked into the library and sat

down at the desk. Next to her, there was a small, grey goat sitting on a seat. Her brows furrowed, but then she realised.

"My sister somehow managed to sneak in using my suitcase, " Sarah stated with a faint amused smile pulling at the edges of her lips. "Can you believe it?"

"Yes, actually, " Asrani, the goat, responded. Suddenly, the grey goat shifted, its features melting into that of a human. Asrani looked at Sarah with still goat-like eyes. Asrani's messy, dark brown hair fell over his eyes and his pale skin shimmered when the sunlight from the window hit him. His tail curled subconsciously around his left leg and his ears perked up. His hand trailed through his hair upwards and then up one of his horns.

"I still don't understand how or why

you gained that power, " Sarah commented. She chuckled, but Asrani looked up at her with a thoughtful expression on his face. There was silence before he asked,

"How exactly did she manage though?"

"She curled up into a ball and fit into my suitcase, " Sarah said matter-of-factually. Asrani's greenish yellow eyes went slightly wider than normal and his eyebrows raised.

"Oh?"

"Yeah. So, what should I do with her?"

"Text your parents and get them to pick that little bundle of unspecified emotions up in their oh-so-new-and-better method of transportation, " He responded dryly. Sarah snorted in amusement.

"Still salty about that, hm?" Sarah asked in a teasing tone. Asrani rolls his eyes in response.

"Do you think we're being watched?" Sarah asked abruptly as she looked around. Asrani raised a singular eyebrow at the sudden question. He visibly thought for a moment; she could see the cogs turning through his eyes which stared at the floor.

"Your paranoia is getting the better of you, " Asrani said, his tone flat and his expression unreadable. Sarah shrugged and tried to brush off the feeling of being watched.

"So...what are you doing here?" Sarah asked. Asrani hummed and looked down at the floor again.

"Research." He responded blankly and she raised an eyebrow at him.

"Research?" she repeated questioningly. Asrani nodded as he looked back up at her.

"What research?" Sarah asked as she tilted her head and narrowed her eyes.

"Is that any of your business, Sarah Woods?" He asked darkly, his facial expression blank and his black lips pressed in a straight line. She shook her head, her eyes went a bit wider than normal. Asrani nodded and his intense gaze softened and returned to the floor. "Good, now what are you doing here?"

"Just signing in, " She stated calmly with a slight smile. He gave her a slight nod of confirmation.

"Like I said, my sister managed to hide in a suitcase. She's thirteen so she could fit, " Sarah said again and he just looked at her.

"You've said that already and I know, " He said with a slight, quiet, breathy chuckle.

She also snickered as a smile crept its way onto her lips.

Death loomed in the shadows as he made sure that his presence remained unknown. Asrani couldn't sense him. Either that or the shape-shifter just didn't care. But one thing for sure, is that Death thought Asrani was suspicious. Perhaps he and his 'God' had something to do with these . . . incidents. He'd have to keep a look out and intervene if necessary...which it probably would be. After he saw the pair get up, Death disappeared into the shadows.

Asrani nodded to his friend as a goodbye.

"Bye!" Sarah called out as Asrani got up and took some darkly coloured books with him.

He paused midway from the door.

"Farewell, " He responded with a soft voice. She nodded and he continued and left, leaving Sarah alone in the library.

Chapter 5

Given

Una had regretted going in her sisters

case, but had no choice but to wait and see what happened. Una knew she couldn't escape and run, even though she really wanted to. She tried to scream for help, but she soon figured out that she would be threatened by Amaris. Una stopped and tried to think of a plan, but all she could come up with was to run away as fast as her legs could take her. Amaris was stronger than her, it would never work. Una's tears started streaming down her tanned, freckled face.

Amaris had never had love from her parents, because they were dead, so she tried to ruin the sister's relationship to help her cope with her insanity. Amaris really wanted her parents so Tori said she'd get her parents if she kidnapped Una. For the ritual that would 'bring her parents back'.

"Why are you doing this to me!?" Una blurts out.

"I'm sick of seeing happy relationships! I want my own for once, and I will get it when the ritual is complete!" she smirks smugly. Una started to cry, she sniffled and wiped her eyes with her arm making her tears drip down her skin.

A voice boomed in the lair.

"Awh a poor child... How old is she Amaris?"

"She's thirteen and a half ma'am!" Amaris said almost immediately. She seemed quite scared of the voice. "She loves her sister with all her heart, apparently, " Amaris said, looking around.

"Could you...Knock her out for me?" The voice said with a dark tone.

"Gladly, " Amaris said as she picked up a metal pipe that was at the side of her and whacked Una on her head. Una fell to the floor with blood dripping down the side of her head.

"Not like that Amaris..."

"Oops my bad!" Amaris shrugged her shoulders and started setting up the ritual.

The door creaked open ever so slightly and appeared to be a historian and scientist standing with a nineteen year old student called Tori - they were all talking quietly so no one could hear them. "Here you are Tori!" Amaris said and brought Una close to her.

"Ah! Thank you so much, " Tori smirked.

Chapter 6

The Rite

Complex looking machines and objects

were scattered around the sides of the circular room. Bright lights pierced your eyes when you enter the room, but you eventually get used to it. The two professors, Mike and Jo, looked confused and like they were preparing themselves to do something horrid. That girl looked ecstatic that Una was there, as if she planned for her to be there.

The student joyfully skipped over to them shaking their hands vigorously.

"The perfect subject, " piped up the girl, "With her valuable, young soul, everyone shall be brought back for good. Amaris, get her in the chains. And by the way, I am Tori, and you girl... Are soon to be dead."

Una kicked and screamed in a blind panic and rage. She tried running out the door but was met with a knife up against her face.

"Sorry, but it's too late to run. I have a job to do, " Amaris told her. Una stepped back, tearing up and slumping down to the floor. She curled up in a ball trying to hide from the frightening scene.

Amaris paced around Una before deciding to pick her up, but Una flailed her arms and legs tried to escape her grasp.

"Stop struggling! It's easier if you go of your own will, " mentioned Amaris. "Stop or I will have to knock you out."

She refused to stop, so Amaris had no choice but to kick her in the face, knocking her out cold and dragging her to the centre of the large pentagram.

In the large centre, there was something in the middle of a red pentagram, the shrine made of dark crystals and electric puddles of blue liquid. The same type used for rituals or sacrifices. The puddles of electrified liquid covered each of the points of the pentagrams star and were connected by streams of purple sparks.

Amaris hoisted Una up into jet black chains with an aura like purple fire, two on her ankles and two on her wrists. At this point, her head and limbs were all facing in the same direction as the sharp points on the pentagram. Una began to get zapped by the great electric streams getting faster and faster till the chains became red with her fresh blood.

"Lets begin, she has been prepared well, " Tori mumbled to the shaken scientist and they powered up the large machines. An intense glow shot out of Una's pores at the glass windows creating an obscure blinding light. Tori was amazed at the sight of this unimaginable power and magical assortment of symbols on the glass.

Una screamed like a wild fox on a cool night. The chains buckled wildly. Tori ordered Mike, the historian, and Jo, the scientist, to tighten the tough chains almost blinding themselves whilst doing so. Una's body stretched and burnt like bread in a two hundred degree oven.

Anyone could've mistook her screams for a huge machine in a factory; they were that loud. The professors looked away in shame because they knew that they are the ones who had caused such misfortune on this girl.

Tori left not wanting to hear the ear piercing screams and hid from the light brighter than the sun and stars themselves.

"Make sure she stays like this for the next few hours. I will inform you when we are ready for initiation two!" Tori shouted over Una's screams.

"Go see if her older sister has noticed anything yet, " commanded Tori. "We don't need her ruining everything for us. Magic will be back in this world and back for good." Amaris nodded and headed out and up the stairs to investigate.

"Now how am I going to inform her I can't bring her parents back?" Tori asked herself.

Chapter 7

Missing

The exciting, informative lecture had

come to a satisfying end and Sarah left the huge lecture hall, trying to find the people she was whispering across the room to. Then she found him. He was trying to get through the tough crowd but he was a short boy, not easily seen by others and almost stampeded by the taller people who had not seen that he was underneath them.

"I can't wait until the next lecture!" she said to one of her new friends, Tatum. In a lively manner, Sarah skipped back to her shared dorm through the loud campus with not a worry on her mind, the buildings were so massive that their gloomy shadows covered almost the entirety of the campus. As Sarah walked the couple hallways and up the few stairs, she suddenly felt gloomy; she started to believe something was indeed wrong. She thought that maybe something bad had happened to Una. Sarah's flatmate came up to her and invited her to a party for the day after, but Sarah declined because she was in a panic because she had to get to her dorm to check on Una. She sprinted to her dorm, worried for Una's sake, expecting the worst.

"Una, I'm home, " Sarah shouted, but there was no response.

Sarah attempted to unlock the door and realised the lock had been tampered with, so she opened the door and the first thing she saw was her unmade bed... something wasn't right. She had made her bed first-thing that morning, before the lecture.

"Hey! stop messing around, where are you? Una?"

When she looked around, the whole place

was covered with her clothes and accessories. She shivered at the thought of somebody searching through her room. Sarah's eyes stopped where her suitcase had been originally left. It was now in the corner of the room. In a panic, she decided to look through everything just in-case something happened to her most valuable possessions but then it hit her . . . "UNA!"

Chapter 8

The Search

Sarah started to panic. She rapidly slammed doors open and shut to see if Una was there. Door after door, after door, she looked, but she could not find her.

"Sorry!" Sarah blurted out, she accidentally opened a door full of classmates. It was really embarrassing for her. Everything became intense and the only thing Sarah could think about was what had happened to her younger sister. Sarah ran everywhere trying to find Una, in other rooms, in the cafe.

To everybody she saw, she asked, "Have you seen my sister, Una?"

She sat down to catch her breath from all the running and sighed, tears streaming down her face. She started to think it was her fault that Una was gone and probably dead. *"This is all my fault, why did I leave her? I'm so stupid!"* she thought. She couldn't shake off the feeling that it was HER fault Una was missing. She wiped the tears from her eyes, but they kept flowing like an ever-falling waterfall, her breathing slowed and the tears stopped as she realised that she had not lost Una and she had not left the dorm...somebody had taken her! Sarah immediately called the police and her friends.

As Sarah put down her phone she ran through the library and people thought it was weird but shrugged it off then went through the English and maths department than ran into a laboratory where there were a couple kids learning Chemistry.

"I'm so sorry just ignore me, " said Sarah in a panic.

"Are you alright?" asked the Chemistry teacher.

"Yea, I'm fine why wouldn't I be I'm in university, " replied Sarah as she ran before the teacher could say anything, *where are you Una, come on your literally the only best friend I have right now I need you.*

Sarah ran all around the campus over and over again and even asked some other kids if they have saw a kid that looked thirteen but none of them did.

"UNA, WHERE ARE YOU? THIS IS NOT EVEN FUNNY ANYMORE I'M GETTING WORRIED NOW!" shouted Una.

Chapter 9

Newsflash

The President and his speech writer prepared to go on World-Wide television by getting Chad into his suit and practising his speech, knowing they both had a long day ahead of them. His assistant reminded him he had one minute before they have to go on live television. The President was very nervous, but he went along with it...

"Chad, it's time!"

President Chad took a few deep breaths until he had to go live and be on camera, he walked up to the camera and told the world about the important news.

"Hello fellow people, how are we? I have some very important news I need to tell you all. There might be a war starting very soon..." President Chad said in a worried voice.

"I am not really sure how I feel about this right now, so feel free to ask any questions to help you guys get a better idea of what exactly is going on in the world today and in the future..." Chad announced.

"What do you mean there will be a war? What countries will be at war?"

"I mean...there will be a war between enemies and there will not be two countries, more like two realms, but I'm not really sure about it all...Anymore questions?" Chad asked to the room of reporters.

"Not sure how to put this, but I'm very sure that some of you are aware of the dead coming out of the grave or just some rotten corpses? I am going to advise you not to approach these people, even if they are your loved ones; these people are not right in the head. These people will attack or even kill, so I advise you to stay at home if you need something you can get what you need - like food, but only if its needed or important.-NO BEAUTY RELATED THINGS!- Be careful, " informed President Chad.

At this point everyone was in a state of panic as the food shopping went crazy.

Chapter 10

Realisation

Amaris felt a weird feeling like something was wrong, so she looked into it more deeply and seriously. Amaris couldn't believe her eyes about what she had figured out about the uncanny disappearances: the pyramids of Giza ended up in Pisa and the leaning tower of Pisa had ended up in Giza, the statue of liberty had traded her torch for a battery-operated torch and the Stonehenge toppled over each other like dominoes. Amaris couldn't help but think she held a big part in all of it. She didn't give up and still kept trying to find out suitable and possible answers to this. She didn't know how to react and her brain hurt from all the stress on her shoulders weighing her down. Amaris couldn't help but think she had a big part in it, however she felt that she'd done good for the person called Tori. She really wanted to see her parents and she really thought Tori could bring them back, since they were conducting a ritual. She did not know how Tori was going to get them back, but she believed with all her heart that they could because after all she had done so much for them she must deserve to see her parents again. Amaris was really excited to meet her parents she loved her mother and father. She wanted to see her parents so badly. She would go see Tori after she went to the Magic Society. She started walking to the Magic Society, knowing a meeting would be held there. She wanted to see if anyone else had noticed what was happening, If anyone had known anyone to come back from the dead yet. She felt smug. Her legs became weak, they hurt her a lot but she continued to walk to the

Society meeting because she had to find out if anyone else had noticed the strange disappearances and changes.

Chapter 11

An Unfamiliar Face

Sarah walked into the Magic Society meeting and spotted Amaris looking smug in the chair she was sitting in. Her heartbeat quickened at the sight of her smug face. Sarah took a deep breath and tried to look away, but she couldn't. She was looking at Asrani who was looking at Amaris' different coloured eyes(One eye colour was as green as grass and one of her eyes was as brown as chocolate) with hatred in his eyes. Sarah thought about Una and then started to shake and worry something unpleasant would happen to her.

Sarah's stomach started to churn and she felt like she was going to vomit. Sarah could feel the vomit coming up in her throat she took a deep breath. She decided not to stress, because the stress was causing the nausea, Sarah didn't know what to do. She stood there like a deer in headlights. Sarah could hear the mumbling of Amaris, but couldn't quite hear it exactly. Sarah looked away, Amaris looked at Sarah. Sarah looked in Amaris's direction then looked back in the other direction. Sarah started to get sweaty and sat back in her wooden chair. She moved her hair out of her face and saw some people walking down the stairs and watched them from afar Sarah found it interesting and mesmerising that she was inside of a magic society meeting. *Well spying on the meeting.* Sarah sighed quietly, thinking about what she would do now. She glanced at Asrani in a worried way."How is this going to help find my sister?" Sarah seemed restless about finding her sister.

"Just wait...Amaris will help, " Asrani was still staring at Amaris with blank expression." We are wasting time!" Sarah said as she nudged Asrani quite hard.

"WILL YOU STOP THAT!" Asrani tried to whisper but it came out as more of a shout.

"What did she do wrong my good 'friend'?" Amaris saw the others entering the magic society.

"Well she keeps talking about her sister being kidnapped!" Asrani said crossing his arms. Amaris looked like she was about to burst out laughing. Asrani gave her a stare and she just stared back at him. Asrani broke the eye contact to greet all the other members of the society.

William walked through the doors and glanced at Amaris who had her legs propped up on the table;She removed her legs from off the table and onto the floor. William nodded in Amaris's direction and turned to Asrani with a frown.

"Why are you here..." William said sounding disgusted.

"I'm part of magic you should know this by now Will."

"Don't call me Will!" Asrani sniggered at William having a strop

"Yeah, Ani, " Amaris had started kicking Asrani under the table. "He doesn't like being called Will"

"OH YOU LITTLE-" The rest of Asrani's sentence trailed off as Amaris kicked him really hard. William smiled at Amaris and she smiled back at him. Sarah stared at Amaris.

"OI!You got a staring problem or what?!"

Sarah shook her head and stared at William instead. Amaris cursed under her breath.

Chapter 12

The Society

Death cloaked himself in a human form

called William and entered the society, shutting the door behind him (it made quite a noise). He looked around, taking in the amount of people, the shiny, epoxy resin floor, the high, black walls, the wooden beams and the large structure of the building. He spotted someone and his expression immediately darkened.

Asrani.

Of course he'd be here! That little worm, Baphomet's little friend. Or slave more like. For a deity so concerned with balance, you would think that he would be against giving out powers and enslaving humans... Since that bleating goat had broken his horn, *he would do anything just to go against Death's wishes.* He was up to something, but he didn't know what.

The two other people he could see were

Amaris and Sarah, but he had no time to exchange pleasantries or think about it too thoroughly. So he decided it would be best to get to the meeting as soon as possible. He arrived a few minutes before it started so he sat down (after scowling at Asrani)on his seat in the meeting room. He had gotten a newspaper to read to try and kill the boredom but he didn't pay attention to it much because his gaze was set on the door. It opens and a few people that didn't matter to his current mission came in. He didn't pay them much attention, his eyes still locked on the door. Waiting. Waiting. Eventually, all of the others arrive and the meeting could finally start.

"The magic has returned!" Asrani said excitedly.

"And my sister is missing!" Sarah exclaimed. Both William's and Asrani's eyes widened. Amaris let out a quiet chuckle.

"Una? Your sister who sneaked her way into the university?" Asrani asked as his eyebrows raise and then furrowed.

"We need to find the root cause of this, " William stated as he gave Asrani a glare. He returned the glare before he broke the eye contact to look at Sarah.

"As much as I hate to admit it Will over here is...Right, " Asrani said as he grimaced, looking like the words tasted bad. He scoffed at the nickname. Amaris stayed watching in the shadows.

"I'm sure you'll find your sister eventually, " Asrani said but his eyes momentarily flickered to William. Sarah nodded but her facial expression looked devastated. He sent her a pitiful look. They turned away from Amaris, leaving her to stare at the back of their heads. She disappeared out of the room, chuckling to herself. Asrani stormed out of the room after her cursing under his breath.

"Why are you chuckling?" Asrani demanded as he grabbed the collar of Amaris' shirt. She dug her hand in her pocket and pulled out a small knife and as soon as she does he whacked her across the face.

"What is wrong with you, you-" Asrani yells but before he could finish she slashed the knife, the blow directed at Asrani's face. Luckily, he jumped back in time so the knife only cut his cheek. His hand reached up to touch the small wound. He held it there for a moment before he pulled his hand back to look at the crimson liquid on his finger. He scowled up at her to which she gave him a crazy grin. He glared at her before regaining his normal composure. He stood up straight and stormed off, going to his room to calm down and be in more of a peaceful place. That was already enough drama then what he would have liked in an already emotionally overwhelming day. William poked his head outside of the room and saw Asrani (with a fresh cut on his face) walk off in a hurry. He decided to follow the shape-shifter.

Chapter 13

Red Herring

William had followed Asrani into his

room, but he hadn't noticed. His gaze was focused on the table where history books sat piled high on his bedside table. On the edge of the desk, two books lay open and the goat-like face of Baphomet stared out blankly. Asrani's pale, long fingers traced the page and he muttered a prayer to his deity under his breath.

William walked up to Asrani and tapped his shoulder to get his attention.

"Yes, what do you need?" Asrani asked, not bothering to hide how annoyed he is by the sudden invasion of his room. They both stared at each other with similarly stern expressions for a few minutes.

"What are you researching?" William asked harshly.

"None of your concern!" Asrani protested defensively.

"Oh shut up; I know you're hiding something!" he insisted.

"I am not hiding anything!" she snapped

"Then why were you at the meeting? Checking to see if your actions caused the chaos you wanted?" William yelled.

"I felt the magic rising too! I know it's been gone for years and I'm just as confused as you are!"

"Liar!" William called as Asrani scoffed with an offended expression.

"You're acting quite childish with all of that name calling, " the shape-shifter stated and William rolled his eyes.

"Oh please! You do it all of the time. You can't say anything, " William resorted to as the shifter groans in annoyance.

William noticed the books that were on his bedside table and desk and his brows furrowed. He studied the cover of the books. They all had an upside down pentagram on them with similar titles. He scoffed with disgust.

"You and your stupid 'god', " William spat. Asrani groaned again as he looked at the books down on his table.

"It's just Baphomet. I don't get why you have such a strong negative opinion of him, " The shifter said as he crossed his arms.

"He's closely linked with Satan. You know, the evil demon thing?" William said as he glared at Asrani with piercing eyes.

"He is not!" The shape shifter argued, "He's a deity allegedly worshipped by The Knights Templar back in 1307! Not Satan!"

"Don't lie to me, " William snapped.

"I'm not!"

"Yes, you are. You say you don't worship Satan but you sure do lie like him."

"NO!"

"No wonder why they set the fire, " Death said coldly.

"Shut up!" Asrani yelled before he punched William across the face in a fit of anger. William's eyes widened and his hand reached up to touch his aching cheek. Asrani sighed again, took a deep breath and his face softened." Sorry, " he mumbled weakly as he looked away.

William cleared his throat and also sighed. "If I hear one more peep about you I swear!"

"Alright alright! Stop with your lectures!" Asrani interrupted.

"The stuff you research is dangerous. If one more thing happens I will get involved, " William said sternly. They both nodded, both looked equally defeated and exhausted. William nodded again in confirmation before he left and slammed the door behind him.

Chapter 14

Gloat

Amaris walked toward Jo, the scientist,

with an excited smile.

"Hey weird dude! I'm pretty sure magic is coming back and corrupting the world..I mean it would explain the weird things going on lately, " Amaris said with a slight grin on hers face that was big enough to be seen by the scientist Jo.

"Will you just shut up..You idiot. I will not allow you to talk about magic

like that. Magic is powerful and not to be messed with!" The scientist said in a mad voice.

"Stop shouting at her will you!" Mike, the historian said in an annoyed voice.

Mike had noticed that Jo's face was red and he had never seen their face so red, so he could tell they were frustrated.

"All you do is shout, shout and shout is that on your to-do list or something because you shout every single day! Shouting is not an appropriate way to handle something and you know that it isn't so why can't you just shut up for once!?" The historian would say." And anyways Amaris is sensitive!" Amaris Was finally paying attention after that sentence.

"Well I'm sorry that I want to shout!I don't see any issue with me shouting so stop nagging me about it and stay quiet!" The scientist would shout loader than earlier.

"OH MY GOD JUST SHUT UP FOR ONCE.!" Amaris would scream

The scientist scoffs at Amaris

"I don't know why you get so mad so easily." Amaris said

"You son of a.." The scientist would say but the historian covered his mouth so he wouldn't finish that sentence.

Amaris started walking out of the room, keeping eye contact with the scientist as if she didn't keep eye contact the scientist might have hit her or sneaked up on her. He was clearly mad at Amaris for bringing up magic and saying that it is slowly corrupting the world.

"What are you looking at?!" The scientist said in a mad voice.

Amaris laughed at how he sounded and she could see that the scientists face was going more red by the minute,

"You know I'm just going to go out of this room don't mind me.." Amaris would say with a smirk on her face.

"Yeah you should go as it looks like he's going to lose his mind if you stay any longer." The historian said whilst trying to hold his laugh in.

Amaris closed the door of the laboratory -making a huge bang that scares the scientist Jo- and starts to go down the long stairs that looked like they was endless, Amaris let out a sigh.

When death noticed Amaris was going somewhere he turned invisible and followed Amaris, but she felt a presence behind her so she turned around but she only saw stairs so she kept on walking down to the ground floor. Amaris heard footsteps and creaking but she didn't turn around. Black liquid rolled down the stairs and brown liquid followed, "Gross did someone have diarrhoea something-probably the scientist-.." Amaris would say to herself. Death lets out a silent laugh and then swears under his breath.

Amaris shouts "Alright who is here, I am not dumb!"

Nobody answered Amaris, Death stood there and tried not to make a noise so he covered his mouth to block himself from making a sound.

"I'm hallucinating...Nobody is here just me by my self." Amaris said in a quiet voice but it sounded like she didn't believe it. Amaris started walking up the long stairs again and Death carried on following her to the bottom of the stairs still shocked that he has made it this far without getting caught by Amaris.

Chapter 15

Confession

Jo and Mike walked around Tori curled

up on the floor and a white beam came from her mouth as her current form melted into a males body;the beam illuminated the whole room. She got back up with huge, feathered white wings that slowly fell behind her. A bright, white glow covered what was once the body of a normal person.

With a booming voice Tori states, "This is who I am. I have hid this for ages. I... am... Gabriel;Angel Gabriel." Mike looked shocked, Jo looked impressed. "I have shown you my true identity and now you mustn't tell anyone or else I will come after you . If you do what I say you'll be safe from my harm ."Gabriel smirked which told nothing but lies.

Mike looks on at Gabriel in shock as he had just witnessed a woman turn into a man (who is an angel,) whilst Jo looked impressed but scared and due to the threat they just nod and agree as to keep themselves safe from harm. They both looked at each other and then back at Gabriel to which he pointed to the exit and orders them to leave. "NOW LEAVE OR ELSE I WILL HAVE TO KILL YOU AND YOU BETTER NOT TELL ANYONE OR ELSE I WILL FIND YOU AND THAT IS NOT A THREAT EITHER!"

"Billions of years ago...before I was me; God and Satan made an agreement that magic shall be wiped off the earth but once I was here I wanted more I am not the first to fall...God and Satan decided that i wasn't fit for looking after heavens gates so he gave that job to...Saint Peter, " Gabriel wrinkled his nose as he said the words '

Saint Peter' "Goody two shoes saint Peter. It's my job to bring magic back once and for all, do you hear me!"

"Y-Yes s-sir" Jo said looking quite scared. They nudged Mike out of his trance

"Hm? OH! UM! Yes sir!" Mike said looking quite stupid. whilst looking on with huge widened pupils that made him look like a toddler that just witnessed their block tower fall over. they both then walked out of the laboratory and looked at each other and nodded and Mike piped up and said " Lets never mention that again."

"Agreed" Jo said whilst looking off into the distance. The pair then look the same way and walk off in silence. with the shape shifting angel just stood floating whilst giving them a death stare from the window.

Chapter 16

The
Confrontation

Amaris ran all around the University looking for Gabriel. She looked in the library, all the Laboratories and even the classrooms. He wasn't there.

"He has to be down in the lair, " she whispered to herself.

She sprinted to the the stairs and then ran down them as fast as she could to the to the bottom and saw Gabriel down by the ritual.

"Where are my parents?" Amaris questioned.

"They are not going to come! I bet they hate you by now! All the mischievous things you've done, " Gabriel said. Amaris doesn't know what to do and looks at Gabriel with anger.

"I'VE done everything for you! I have

brought her to the ritual and all!" said Amaris, "YOU HAVE TO GIVE ME MY PARENTS, I BEG YOU!" Surprisingly, Amaris punched Gabriel so hard she broke her fist and Gabriel's nose was all bruised up and swollen. Gabriel just laughed and pushed Amaris into the area where the ritual is going to take place. Gabriel laughed, "Amaris you can't get everything in life, It's how the world works!" Mike looked devastated by the words that came out of Gabriel's mouth. Jo looked unimpressed and shook their head whilst they stood there quietly waiting for the ritual to start. Gabriel smirked and told Amaris to sit down. Amaris obliged and sat down by force from Gabriel pushing her shoulders down towards the floor. Slowly and carelessly, Gabriel knelt down next to her.

"HEY GABRIEL WHAT HAPPENED TO OUR DEAL!" she shouted as she clenched her fists so much that her nails dug into her skin. She swung her hand and punched Gabriel, knocking him back.

"You've got power haven't you?" Gabriel stated calmly as he got knocked back.

"Yeah, well you should have held your end of the deal then I wouldn't have had to do that!" yelled Amaris. Gabriel laughed, stood up and brushed the dirt off them.

"You need to calm down, Amar, " Gabriel said in a low whisper.

"DON'T CALL ME AMAR!" Amaris snapped.

"I can call you what I want!" Gabriel replied angrily.

"Ok then, GABE, " Amaris said. Gabriel scowled at the name. They pushed Amaris backwards with invisible force making her cough, blood spluttered on the ground.

"You promised that I could have my parents back! I helped you! I did all of this for you and then you don't hold up your end of the deal! All these years, I have been treated differently, not respected, called names, this is all because I have no parents! Please Gabriel, I'm begging you! I just want to feel the love from my parents and have a childhood..." Amaris said with a mix of great anger and great sorrow. *The anger bubbling inside of her recalled the day when someone wouldn't let her buy food from the canteen saying:*

"Hey, orphans can't buy food they can't get any money from their parents, " the bully taunted.

"How stupid are you? Have you ever

heard of benefits?" said Amaris before she
punched him in the face. Amaris tried to
explain to the teachers why she did it but
they were having none of it.

"That's why i want my parents, so that
I won't be treated so differently, " said
Amaris

"I can't I'm so sorry I wish I could!
But I literally can't do it" said Gabriel
solemnly.

"And you're only telling me this now?
So you used me to get what you wanted
and I thought you were the good one!"
yelled Amaris who saw red.

"The reason I can't do it is because it
is currently an unavailable option for me; I
lied to God and if I bring your parents back
down to Earth out of The Heavens then
he will know about this entire operation,

" stated Gabriel.

I new they couldn't be trusted, I'm so stupid she thought as she stormed off.

"Amaris don't be like that, " said Gabriel.

"OH WILL YOU JUST SHUT UP, I DON'T WANT TO SPEAK TO YOU OR ANYONE FOR THE TIME BEING!" yelled Amaris.

Amaris stormed out of the lab yelling unholy things towards Gabriel stomping up the many flights of stairs like a child having a 'strop' or a 'tantrum' but way worse. She reached the top of the smooth stairs heading towards the quiet library, the perfect place to sneak up on someone unsuspecting. She searched the library's rows and rows of books, eventually finding someone. A boy in a hoodie and jeans reading a book, around 6'1 and seems like the type that wont make a fuss. Amaris took her knife and brought it to the boys pale neck. "I'm sorry." Amaris whispered as she slashed, but the boy wasn't where he just was instead he was behind her. But it wasn't, him. It was a large figure in a cloak or robe with a hood. He stood around 7 feet tall, he had no flesh he had no skin, all he was. Was bones. "Hello Amaris, I am Death."

"Amaris I'm just going to be honest here but no matter how many people you kill or even if you conquer the world, nothing and I mean nothing is going to bring back your parents, " stated Death.

"Oh thanks for that death that's really helpful, " said Amaris sarcastically.

"But you know I'm right though. How about you help me stop Gabriel's whole operation?" Death offered.

"So your basically saying to back-stab Gabriel? Won't that make me worse than him; like the saying two wrongs don't make a right?" asked Amaris

"No, he is the one in the wrong; he decided to lie to you, " said Death.

"Okay, I'll help you, " said Amaris, "But is it true that my parents can't really come back." Death nodded and walked away, Amaris started to tear up, but managed to keep her emotions sealed away.

Chapter 17

A Familiar Face

Amaris put her knife away, *Should I hug or shake hands with him? Why is he so nice to me? Maybe he could be a father-*

figure to me. Should I ask if he could be my father? No I already have a father (although I don't see him). Ugh Amaris snap out of it.

"So do we shake hands or not?" Amaris said debating whether Death would respond or not.

"After we sort Gabriel out, then we shall shake hands, " He said. Amaris nodded then attempted to walk away but Death grabbed her sleeve and said in a hushed tone "WE are going to set this right..." Amaris looked at Death

"Get off my sleeve, " She said. She grabbed death's hand and shoved it off her sleeve. "I'm going to look for Una's sister, " she added. She stormed off leaving Death alone in the library *'Well that was easy'* Death heard a muffled scream and then silence *'I better sort that out'* He thought.

After Amaris had finished relieving her stress, she started looking for Sarah. When She looked in the library, she found Sarah sleeping on a desk with an empty coffee cup. Amaris pulled out her knife again, but she put it back in her pocket realising Death would probably kill her if she killed Sarah because she has already killed a lot of people.

"Wake up lazy, it's your first day!" Amaris said half enthusiastically, trying to be funny.

"No leave me alone!" Sarah muttered.

"Listen if you don't wake up your sister will be DEAD!" Amaris said, shaking Sarah awake.

"WHAT? WHY DIDN'T YOU TELL

ME BEFORE!" Sarah yelled looking at Amaris and admiring the purple half of her hair but then focusing back on Amaris' face.

"I...uh... saw who took your sister!" Amaris said this while crossing her fingers behind her back. She uncrossed her fingers and held out her hand and offered to help Sarah out of her seat but she was already up and her bag was on her back ready for the search to find her sister. "Listen you need to focus because my...Enemy, Is not somebody you should be messing with, " Amaris said as she shook Sarah so she was awake a bit more. Sarah looked at Amaris's pocket to see a knife poking out of her pocket.

"Self defence, " She said before Sarah could ask, "People are always hurting other people now, " Amaris said as she took the knife out and started cleaning it with her shirt which left blood on her clothes.

"I'm guessing somebody tried to kill you?" Sarah asked.

"You could say that..."

Chapter 18

Insanity

As she looked down Una noticed that

her skin was turning a pale grey, She felt dizzy and tired and couldn't move. She felt like she was slowly losing her sanity. But then the world around her faded and the sky became a clear blue.

"Where am I?" wondered Una out loud, surprised at how she got from being part of a ritual to being in the middle of a road surrounded by field.

"You are in Rome, " said a mysterious voice behind her.

"Rome?" said Una and she turned around and saw a man. she remembered something from her history class last year; /em The roman empire originated in Rome and is one of the most well known empires

"Yes, the capital of the great roman empire."

"How did I get here?"

"I don't know, you just appeared in front of me, " said the man with a laugh.

"Oh, who are you?"

"I am Hostius, a humble trader, " revealed Hostius

"Hello Hostius, I am Una."

"Hello Una, would you like to come with me on my travels?"

"Okay Hostius, maybe I will find out how I got here on the journey."

So as Hostius and Una rode down the path, on the cart Hostius was driving, they stopped to check on the wheels and to feed the horse pulling the cart. Whilst Una was feeding the horse one of the apples that the trader had on his cart, she noticed a small temple-like structure on a field in the distance and she felt a sudden urge to go to it.

"Hostius, " she asked "Can we go over there?"

"I would not do that if I were you, " He replied in a slightly scared tone.

"Why not?"

"Because it is said to be haunted by a ghost that protects a sacred text."

"I don't believe that, " Said Una being sceptical

"If you do not believe that it is haunted, you may go ahead and take a look but do not take too long because it will be night-fall soon and you don't want to be there at night." Said Hostius with a shudder.

Una walked, at a slightly swifter pace than normal, towards the lone standing temple-like structure in the middle of the field. Once she was within touching distance, she noticed that some of its bricks

were on the verge of falling out and that
a door-like entrance was jutting out of the
structure. She walked over to the entrance,
and she spotted that there was a door handle. with all her effort she pushed down
on the stiff handle and the door opened
even though Una did not push it open, as
if it wanted her to go inside and had been
expecting her. The inside of the temple
was a cave full of cobwebs, dust, old scrip-
tures, but, most importantly, there was an
engraving on the far wall. It was in a different language.

Una realised that in ancient Rome they
did not speak English, that means that
she has been speaking (and understand-
ing) another language and that she could
read what it said engraved into the wall,
it said...

Chapter 19

The Inquiry

"This cabinet meeting has started, "

The President, Chad, announced to the people around him. "My top scientists have figured out that a mysterious energy has caused all of the changes to the world and has originated from a university in Boston, I need your help in deciding if we should let this be or if we should go and investigate this university. If you think we should investigate this university say: aye."

"Aye!" everybody in the room answered.

"Lets go then!"

They look around the university but cannot find anything wrong with it and no magic was found.

"I found something, boss!" A scientist screams out from a nearby forest.

The other scientists come to check out what he had found, they noticed a trace of magic and symbols that nobody could understand. "The symbols look very complicated to understand?" one of the scientists say curiously.

"I'll get the General to search the university for more magic patterns. Please all of you, stay put, " The president said.

The scientists stay where they are being careful to not touch the patterns.

The president called the General to the university to look around-

"Alright boys go and search the university and don't leave any stone un-turned, " Said the General.

"Wait I didn't say to look at stones I said to look for an ener-" Said President Chad getting interrupted.

"I know what you said, President, and that's not what it means. Alright, I'm going to search the university for the source and your either coming with me or your staying right there, " said the General.

"Because you will probably send a nuke and kill the entirety of Russia or something like that, " the General added, muttering under his breath.

The General and President Chad walked into the University and instantly the people there ran up for a signature.

"What do they wan, " Whispered President Chad.

"Oh my god President we've went through this a million times, they just want a signature, d" Whispered the General.

"Well General, tell them to go away; we have some important business to attend, " Said President Chad.

"Alright people move along the Presi-

dent has got to attend some business, dd"
Said the general.

"Thank you" Said President Chad.

"Hey General we have searched the place
from top to bottom, " Said one of the
many soldiers.

"Do I have to do everything myself, you
guys don't even do anything" Said President Chad.

"I mean would it hurt to do something
for once" The General muttered under his
breath

"Did you say something General" Said
President Chad

"No nothing at all" Said the General
replying as fast as he could.

"I'm so confused, I mean where else could
it be" Said President Chad

"It's okay President let just go back to

the white house and see what else is happening and see what is up with these dead vicious corpse's" Said The General.

President Chad and the General both walked away to their cars and drove off into the distance.

Chapter 20

In Tongues

Una looked different. She looked ill and

tired like she had seen a ghost. Sarah ran over to her sobbing, but Mike, the historian, had noticed Una staring at him with a thousand yard stare that soldiers at war would experience. She was muttering something under her breath that sounded like dying lizards.

Mike had heard something similar on one of his trips to an old historic cave which was said to have housed a crazed warlock that went mad after a supposed ritual went wrong. All over the cave walls there had been weird symbols in an ancient language that the tour guide had tried to translate but she said she couldn't and said she was speaking tongues, but he couldn't figure out what it was.

Mike rushed to the library and hovered his finger over every book till he found the one he needed, the book he had read over 100 times so as he flipped to page six hundred and fifty it had a Latin translation page and the words actually read *dies iudicii veniet* which translated to judgement day will come. He ran faster than he could comprehend back to the two girls who had stopped hugging but Una still stared at Mike laughing and getting louder she said again and again *dies iudicii veniet, dies iudicii veniet, dies iudicii veniet* till it grew into a vicious roar. Then she started foaming at the mouth and her eyes rolled back and she collapsed to the floor shaking violently still trying to chant the Latin text, but it turned more into a broken cry that sounded recorded and fake. She was choking and her mouth was gasping for air. That was until she had thrown up, but in-

117

stead of vomit, a grey metal like substance that looked and behaved like mercury was forced out of her mouth.

"That is not meant to happen, " Sarah and Mike both said in unison.

Chapter 21

The Translation

he

Mike started to figure out what Una's ramblings meant and why she went missing because earlier that day Amaris was teasing him and Joe about how magic was coming back, so Mike quickly got up of the floor grabbed his things, but as he was about to exit the room but Una started speaking Latin again so he grabbed his phone and went straight to voice translate and clicked on the Latin setting and after a minute or two the translation Latin 'judgement day will come the dead will rise, the sinners will burn' but the second she said that the building shook and a loud bang echoed through the city. The historian and the scientist looked out of the window to see a large crater and hear the whistle of bombs and a scream of a skuka diving down to bomb a street near by, the roman cavalry were fighting the British Celts. And after Mike and Joe stepped back from the window Una started to speak again but this time she said *bella repetam* and mike instantly knew what Una was saying she was saying 'wars will repeat' so he rushed Joe and himself out of the building leaving una alone in the building and they ran for Gabriel's lair. but as they left a king tiger tank rolled across the middle of campass

and as mike looked left a massive hole the size of a mini bus was blown through the entrance of the university but as Jo looked up they saw a dog fight between a Messerschmit bf109 and a submarine spitfire mk2 end when the German plane came crashing towards the tank whilst a trail of smoke a fire followed it Mike and Jo jumped put of the way into a near by shrub were they watched the small mushroom cloud from the explosion soon faded mike then spotted an exit and darted to it but then a horde of viscous un-dead people and as the pair bith were surounded by the corpes that somehow walked again but as hey looked around they saw una near the hole from the tank add something else to her screams:" *Nos omnes in occursum nostri finis!*" they look back at the horde and see gap and they run whilst jumping and swerving past the walking dead

Chapter 22

The War Of Wars

A TV blared in the corner. A news-reporter, sat in the middle of the screen in a grey suit, he mentioned people were starting to panic because of the news that had travelled around about the world about battle of Somme restarting, it happened almost 108 years ago with well over one-million casualties! Some of the people that visited the place where The Battle Of Somme took place are now either injured or have died.

The TV presenter came back in a flash and stated that the current Normandy police spotted what looked like fake blimps and people in grey army uniform setting up guns and tanks near or in the bunkers that used to be used in World War 2 and old rusty landing crafts are landing on Omaha beach.

Another TV presenter announced that another tectonic plate has formed in the Earth's core. People at first were worried about it, especially geologists because of the random tectonic plate that had formed. Most people have got used to the changes that Earth had made. Some people still believe that it is wrong and haven't got used to it at all.

In Germany, many people have spotted Nazi soldiers, but the sightings have been near a pub so the police didn't take the people serious until someone was found dead in their house with a bullet wound from a MP40 which was used in WW2 by the Nazi soldiers.The German army saw about 40 million half rotten soldiers in Nazi uniforms with guns.

Archaeologists were over the moon because the pyramids have opened and they can see what the Pharaoh's have been buried with and learn so much more about ancient Egypt, but on the other hand people in Mexico are going missing with no trace left.

The people are getting worried in France, since the Panzer-Elite have taken over France with their tanks and artillery and the French army couldn't get close enough to get a negotiation.+

All the wars came crashing in. In a panic everyone feared for their lives and stayed inside their houses. With petrified faces, everyone cried solitarily scared for their lives.

Meanwhile, Amaris was strolling down the street with no fear of being shot or killed as she was immune.

"God! This is like christmas shopping last minute!" Amaris stopped in her tracks to stare at some Nazi's confused about road signs. She placed a hand on her hip and continued walking.

Chapter 23

Haywire

Una felt as if she was losing herself.

Una tried to hold on to her childhood memories, but she was failing. Una missed her sister, Sarah, and her parents. She wished she could hug her again. She hoped she'd be with Sarah again soon. The voices in Una's head were taking over her, she had no choice but to give in. Una's head started to go crazy, The voices in Una's head started to ask questions like "is Sarah going to come save me". Una wanted to be free, not trapped like an animal in a cage. Una started to hit and throw things. Una wished she didn't go with Sarah in the suitcase. Una regretted her decision even though she did want to be with her sister, Sarah. Una just doesn't understand why Amaris would want to kidnap her, she wanted to know why. Una thought of ways to escape every day, and none of the plans worked, no matter what she tried and how many times she tried they just never worked, she started to give up hope but Una thought to herself "no, im going to do this.. for me and my sister". Una began to cry, it looked like a waterfall but then it started to looked like a lake, Una's tears dribbled all the way down to her elbows. Una felt so many feelings: rage, fear and distress. Una eventually took all of her anger out on Amaris, Una shouted at Amaris. Una pleaded Amaris to let her go but Amaris wouldn't listen, Amaris didn't care about what Una had to say. Una knew she had to ask Amaris about why Amaris kidnapped her..

"Amaris, why did-d you-u kidnap-p me?" Una asked in nervousness.

"I can't tell you. if I tell you, you'll ruin

everything!". Amaris replied.

"But Una, why did you ask?". Amaris asked, looking confused.

"Because I just wanted to know.." Una replied.

Amaris couldn't help but feel bad, but she knew she couldn't stop, because if she stopped she would look weak. Una looked so drained and hurt, Una's clothes were ripped and they were hanging off her skin. Una had bruises all over her body, she looked in pain and uncomfortable. Una prayed and wished every day that Amaris would let her free or her sister, Sarah would come save her. Una thought everything was all her fault, but not all of it was.. it was mostly Amaris's fault. Amaris wanted to take away the sisterly love between Una and Sarah (Even though sister love can

never ever end, no matter what happens)
Amaris was jealous because she doesn't
have a sister. Amaris doesn't understand
the stress she's putting everyone through.

"I can't take this anymore, i'm going to
escape.. tonight" Una thought.

Una planned how she was going to escape until Amaris fell asleep.

When Amaris was sleeping, Una made
sure Amaris was actually asleep before Una
made the big decision if she should (try)
and escape. Una is already a step ahead
of Amaris.

Once Una knew Amaris was deffinetly
sleeping.. Una tip-toad to the spot Una
had planned to escape from, A hole in the
wall, Una crawled all the way through..
until she reached the exit, it looked dusty
and dirty. it smelt like moldy cheese, it

was a horrible place to be in.. But Una was just so happy to finally be free, she was so excited to see her sister again after so long.

Amaris woke up.. she was now outside, with Una. Una ran as far as possible. Una panted and was out of breath but Una didn't want to give up, so she didn't give up.. for herself, and Sarah. Una ran and ran until she didn't know where she was. Tall trees surrounded Una, the grass was as green as brocoli. Una didn't know which way to go, she could go left or right, or maybe even dig a hole to go underground.. or Una could just stay in the centre.

Una stayed still for a minute and thought "Left doesn't seem like the correct way to go and let's definitely not go under ground, so my only decision left is to go.. right"

So that's what she did.. she travelled right. And again Una ran and ran until she was out of breath and couldn't run anymore.

Una was now at a place she was familiar with, but she couldn't quite work out exactly where it is or what the place is called.

Una's phone was dead so she couldn't call Sarah. A sweet looking women walked past. "Hi dear, What are you doing outside on your own?" the women asked in a sweet voice.

"Uh Hi. i'm just waiting for my sister, she's in that corner shop over there!" Una pointed sharply to the direction of the corner shop.

Una knew that her sister wasn't in the

creepy corner shop, in fact Una didn't at
all know where Sarah was, she just said it
to make sure the women wouldn't worry.

Chapter 24

The Encounter

"I should've stayed in teaching... like

I'm all up for an adventure but this, now this, is too much" said Mike with a sigh as he looked at Jo past the scientific instruments and all the books on the shelves that were gathering dust.

"Don't look at me, I just wanted to stay in my lab with my test tubes and all my other scientific instruments, that you would not Understand." said Jo with a chuckle. They both heard a 'thump!' so they both ran into the second room (which was the small room where the entrance to the lair was) to see where the loud thump had come from and, to their surprise, they stumbled across Sarah, Amaris and Asrani.

"You shouldn't be in here, it is too dangerous." said Mike.

"One of the crystals could explode or

you could get killed by a blast of mystic energy that she expelled, it's just not safe." Said Jo agreeing with Mike.

"We are here to save my sister, where is she?" said Sarah in a stern voice.

"Tell us where she is, or else." demanded Amaris as slightly unsheathed her knife to show Jo and Mike what would happen if they didn't tell them where Una was.

"She, " Jo said in a smaller voice than before "Is in the next room, but you should not go in there because..."

"We don't care if it isn't safe, we are going to get Sarah's sister back!" Stated Asrani as he transformed into a black jaguar and snarled viciously at Jo and Mike and they both stumbled back out of the way of the entrance.

"Lets go get my sister back..."

As soon as Sarah said that, everyone jumped as the door burst open and Gabriel and Death walk through, arguing, and everyone thinks at the exact same time that: *We should not be here.*

Chapter 25

'Oops'

Mike had started pacing up and down

because of how hot and loud it was, when all of a sudden then there was a big bang as the doors burst open. Everyone turned to look and saw Death and Gabriel shouting at each other, blaming each other for what had happened. Mike sensed a fight and got prepared.

"GET READY DEATH AND GABRIEL ARE ABOUT TO FIGHT!" shouted Mike with a shake in his voice.

Death and Gabriel continued to argue. Meanwhile, on the roof, President Chad stepped out of his presidential helicopter with a few agents with guns. They ran down the five flights of stairs to the lair. The thudding of the agents running down the stairs thundered above their heads. *What could it actually be?* Mike thought.

President Chad ran through the door.

Death pulled his scythe and threatened to slice one of Gabriel's wings off, but then Gabriel punched Death in the face and made him go to the ground. Death grabbed his scythe and swung it. A deep gash appeared on Gabriel's left cheek and a mercury-like substance ran down his face.

"You just got lucky with that! You're dead now!" said Gabriel, while wiping the substance off his face.

"You fool! How can you kill Death, Gabriel? But I know you can kill an angel!" Death laughed maniacally, raising his scythe to Gabriel's neck.

"Fallen Archangel, " Asrani corrected from the opposite side of the room. Death scoffed.

Mike, Joe, Sarah, Amaris and Asrani all charged at Gabriel to help Death, meanwhile President Chad ran to cover and pulled out his gun and started randomly shooting. It nearly hit people, until one of the bullets hit a dark purple crystal in the middle of the circle and shattered it! The shards went everywhere.

"You're going to reset the universe!" said Gabriel.

"Did I do that?" asked the President, confused.

"YES!" Shouted the entire lair.

"Oops." said The President Chad, but nothing happened until...an explosion!

A massive white explosion covered the room and all eternity was sucked into a void where there was no sound at all just a green dot...

Chapter 26

Epilogue

All was white.

Gabriel and Death looked around and everyone, everything had disappeared. There was nothing except the two of them. They looked around and met each other's gaze, their brows furrowed and their eyes narrowed. Death was the first to speak.

"This is all your fault, " he said with a small smirk that was just large enough for Gabriel to see.

They replied with anger rising in their voice, "It's not my fault that you had to stop me from something that would have changed the earth for the better."

"FOR THE BETTER?!" Death remarked with a sneer. "It would have disrupted the balance of life and death forever and apparently that is just what happened judging by the look of this void-like abyss all around us."

"I DID NOT KNOW THIS WOULD HAPPEN!"

"YES, YOU DID! YOU JUST LIED THEN BECAUSE YOU KNEW 'HE' WOULD BE LISTENING!"

"OF COURSE I DID BECAUSE 'HE' WILL KILL ME AND YOU!" They shouted, but as they did so a bright, powerful light appeared in front of them and got bigger and bigger until it was covering all of the void in front of them and said, in a powerful booming voice, "WHO IS RESPONSIBLE FOR THIS DISASTER!"

Death and Gabriel both point at each other like two toddlers blaming each other.

Printed in Great Britain
by Amazon

36804446R00088